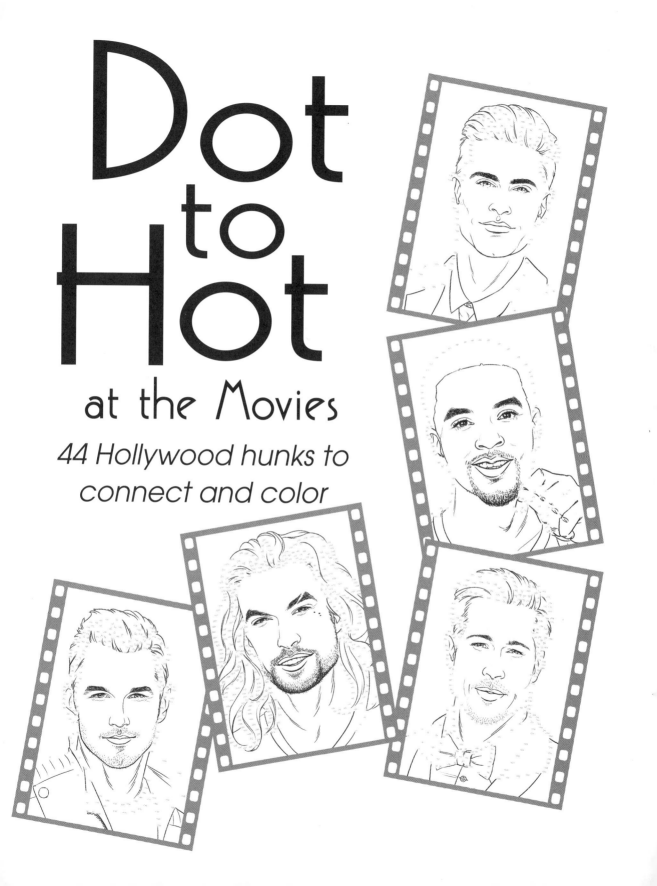

Dot to Hot

at the Movies

44 Hollywood hunks to connect and color

A creative dot-to-dot book with a cinematic twist!
Dot to Hot at the Movies stars dozens of dot-to-dot Hollywood heartthrobs
from Hemsworth and Jackman to Elba and Redmayne.

From hunks and heroes to rebels and bad boys, these hot Hollywood hunks
are all waiting to be lovingly completed by you!

Chris Hemsworth

Sapphire eyes. Blonde. Tall. Did we mention the godlike biceps? The most dazzling of movie-star good looks? The fact that he's walked straight out of the outback and can also surf, box, and ride a motorcycle? Whether he's playing a hammer-throwing alpha god or a hard-drinking Formula One racer, Chris Hemsworth is pretty much the manliest man in Hollywood. And then, just when he couldn't seem any more perfect, he goes and calls himself a feminist who loves strong, funny women, and is also happy playing a receptionist in an all-female *Ghostbusters* or a fairy-tale huntsman who gets rescued by women. Chris, stop it! It's too much. . . .

Idris Elba

Six foot three inches of good-looking, square-shouldered man power, Idris Elba is the hot, tough-guy actor of the moment. He has rocketed from London to Hollywood, worked nights at a car factory, and done his time as a shop clerk and a DJ before he bought himself a ticket to New York and landed a role in *The Wire*. Elba's got the stare, the sex appeal, and the deep, gravelly voice, and whether he's playing a drug lord or detective, he's the smart one who can outwit those around him. And he can put his hand to pretty much anything: Heimdall, the Asgardian god; Mandela, the hero who brought down apartheid; a cockney sea lion called Fluke; and who knows? He may even be the next Bond.

Hugh Jackman

He's ruggedly handsome with an amazingly muscular physique (often plus claws). To sum him up in one word: hunky. But versatile hunky. Jackman can be a superhero in *Wolverine*, can be romantic in *Kate & Leopold*, can do historical drama in *Australia,* and, yes, he can EVEN SING (check out *Les Misérables*). He's also a dancer, producer, and multi-instrumentalist. And if that doesn't sound like enough to have you swooning, he's also a real-life hero—he saved his children and another man from a riptide. No wonder *People* magazine has chosen him as one of the 50 Most Beautiful People in the World five times!

Jason Statham

This is the man with the stare, the gravelly voice, and the body of steel . . . but it's more than that. Jason Statham is the real deal. He started out working in a street stall, then became a model before hotfooting it over to Hollywood and turning into an action hero. He always performs ALL of his own stunts. He can do his own car chases, jump off tall buildings, and look like he means it in a fight. Yes, you've got it, Jason Statham is a self-made, hard-hitting, seriously sexy, real-life action hero. And in case you were thinking he might take himself too seriously, you should see *Spy*. Yes (swoon), he's funny, too.

Ryan Gosling

Say his name and you'll sigh. Or get giddy. Or squeak. He has that kind of effect on people. He's got baby-blue eyes, washboard abs, a feline prowl . . . we could go on, but really he's just so, so watchable. Especially in *The Notebook* (in which he pulls off possibly one of the most famous smooching scenes in movie history). It's no wonder he has gone from an all-singing, all-dancing, Disney kid to the dizzy heights of *La La Land* on his own terms. He's shown off his versatility in musical romantic comedy, political drama, slow-burning indie films, and edgy thrillers. And he's just as versatile offscreen. He likes to box and make furniture. He's an accomplished jazz guitarist and singer. Sigh. Squeak. Sigh.

Tom Hiddleston

This guy has looks and brains: He went to Eton and studied at Cambridge. He's a bit of a thespian (this man knows his Shakespeare). Then he turns up as the slick, cunning villain, Loki, in one of the biggest franchise films of the decade, looking sexy in spandex, and suddenly he's off-the-charts famous. Known for his self-deprecating charm and incredibly nifty dance moves (if you haven't already, search "Tom Hiddleston dancing" on the Internet NOW), Tom is the guy you could take home to charm your gran. He's swoonsome, sophisticated, handsome, clever . . . okay, this is the guy your gran would probably fight you for with her knitting needles. He's also the winner of Britain's 2016 Rear of the Year Award. Enough said?

Benedict Cumberbatch

Known as the thinking girl's hottie and often topping the charts for the Sexiest Man Alive, Benedict is a brilliant actor who never seems to have coveted his fame. Nominated for more theater awards than most people have had hot dinners (not strictly true, but you get the idea), he stumbled across worldwide recognition with *Sherlock*, then turned up the heat in Hollywood by being awe-inspiring in *The Imitation Game* and stealing the show in *Star Trek Into Darkness*. Despite having a zillion female fans, he has not yet played a romantic lead (come on, Ben!). He does a huge amount for charity, rides a motorcycle, and isn't above making jokes at his own expense. Swoon!

Michael Fassbender

There's a lot to love about Michael Fassbender (or "Fassy" as he's known to his friends). He's a MASSIVELY talented actor. Unafraid to explore darkness, he's tackled the roles of a battling Spartan, a hunger striker, a sex addict (full frontal nudity in that one), an android, and a sadistic slave owner. He's amazingly focused (directors love him), he's popular on set (fellow cast members sing his praises), and he's at the top of every casting director's wish list. He's got Irish charm by the bucketload. But that's all slightly missing the point. You see, he has that certain *je ne sais quoi*. That distractingly, delicious, mysteriously, seriously sexy thing. Yes you do, Fassy, you really do. . . .

Donald Glover

This guy is more than a little bit talented. He started out writing for *30 Rock* and worked as a stand-up comedian, so that's his smart and funny credentials sorted. He's a Grammy-nominated rap star (AKA Childish Gambino) and if that doesn't sound like enough, he's got his own TV series, *Atlanta*, which is fresh, funny, totally amazing, and the hot one-to-watch at the moment. Did we also mention that he's GORGEOUS? He's got this hipster-cool vibe and a smile that makes you go weak at the knees. Interested? Well, the good news is that Donald will be playing Lando Calrissian in the Han Solo film. Bring it on, Donald. We want to see more of you. Much more . . .

Zac Efron

Total, all-singing, all-dancing heartthrob. That pretty much sums up Zac Efron. Magnetic blue eyes. Boyish charm. Great hair. Fab abs. He shot to stardom as the teen-dream, pop-culture poster boy. BUT NO MORE. He's reinvented himself through Zac-com, his very own brand of himbo comedy seen in *Neighbors, Mike and Dave Need Wedding Dates,* and *Baywatch*. And we're VERY grateful for it, especially as he seems more than happy to bulk up for new roles (and sport an insane amount of muscle). So now Zac is funny AND beautiful. And if he's reinvented himself once, he can probably do it again. We predict A-list hero status is probably next. #gozac #weareherefor you #everystepoftheway

Mark Wahlberg

He shot to fame with his band, the Funky Bunch (this guy can rap), and then moved on smoothly to Hollywood in the amazing *Boogie Nights* (in which you get to check out pretty much all of Mark), before playing a series of all-American, salt of the earth heroes. Mark basically perfected the strong and silent type, probably because he's got that feeling about him—as if he's one of us, the man of the people (even if he is currently ruling the dizzy heights of Hollywood). Then, just when you might start thinking he takes himself too seriously, he goes and undercuts it all with some box office gold comedy and turns himself into a supercharged Hollywood star. Anything else to mention? Only those Wahlbergian good looks . . .

Alexander Skarsgård

Who could forget Eric the vampire? Skarsgård made 1,000 years of being a Viking vampire look seriously, seriously attractive. The black singlet, leather jacket, and penchant for evil helped. Also the large amount of screen time where he appeared brooding and topless, and for those that were paying attention, his ability to raise his left eyebrow quizzically. Then he swung into Hollywood to get his pecs out again in *Tarzan* and HOORAY! It looks like Skarsgård is on our screens to stay. He's beautiful (tall with piercing eyes and razor-sharp cheekbones), and he's done enough European art house films so you can also feel intellectual as you adore him.

Chris Pine

For the uninitiated, this is the next generation Captain Kirk we're talking about here. But for an A-lister, Chris Pine is also curiously under the radar. A Hollywood heartthrob for those that like them elusive. His next big role is playing Wonder Woman's boyfriend, which suggests he's an action hero without the ego. And although Pine has a fitness regime that would scare Hulk Hogan, he also reads a lot and raves about his passion for interior design. What's more, there's lovely footage of him shedding a tear at the Oscars, so you could say he's very in touch with his emotions. Think Mr. Hunksome meets Mr. New Age Man in near-perfect physical form. Swoooooooon.

Matt Bomer

Drop-dead gorgeous. Chiseled features (like he was sculpted by Michelangelo). Piercing blue eyes. Even straight men gush about Matt Bomer. He's suave and sophisticated in *White Collar*, blush-making in *Magic Mike* (having a bad day? Stressed about work? Watch Matt's strip dancing routine on YouTube. It's better than a cup of hot chocolate), and he's all debonair and double-breasted in F. Scott Fitzgerald's *The Last Tycoon*. But Matt is more than just a pretty face. He's devastating in *The Normal Heart* playing a man dying of AIDS, and his next role is as a trans woman, so this is an actor not afraid to push the boundaries of his craft.

John Boyega

Boyega's career went into hyperdrive when he took on the role of Finn in the new Star Wars films. But it wasn't like getting the role was easy—the auditioning process took SEVEN MONTHS before they decided Boyega was the chosen one. And boy did they choose well. Boyega's screen presence is like a force awakening (okay, okay, I will stop with the bad Star Wars puns). Boyega's dad wanted him to be a preacher, but instead he went to acting school and never looked back. Smart, funny, and stylish, Boyega is one to watch. And for those of us who spotted him first in *Attack the Block*—yeah, he's ours really.

Nikolaj Coster-Waldau

It's very hard to think of him as Nikolaj. I mean obviously, really, he's Jaime Lannister from *Game of Thrones*—arrogant and a bit evil, but with plenty of hidden depths. His skill as an actor? He can make us hate/love/hate/love him without getting tired of him, no matter how many people he pushes out of a window. It probably helps that he's handsome in that ultra-manly, ride-my-big-horse-into-battle-and-win way. And while he does all that, you can admire his lovely cheekbones and his brooding dark brown eyes. We could talk about the fact that he is a devoted husband and father, but no, really we just want to think of him as Lord Commander of the Kingsguard; sexy-bad, but with a hint of redemption.

Chris Evans

Wholesome, handsome, all-American boy next door with his blue eyes and his square jaw and his navy blue spandex suit with the silver star and his round shield . . . what's not to love? Plus the fact that he's also an awe-inspiring supersoldier who goes around saving the world from evil. Oh, okay. That's not Chris Evans. That's actually Captain America. But the trouble is he really looks the part and really inhabits the role, so it's actually quite hard to tell them apart. All the time you're gazing at him, you're wanting to dress up in wartime clothes (think pleated skirt, cinched waist, and fetching feather hat) just so Captain Evans can come and rescue you. I mean Chris America. You know who I mean.

Jamie Foxx

Real name Eric Bishop, Jamie Foxx is so cool, he needs that extra
"x" at the end of his name. If you like your Hollywood heartthrobs
multi-talented, then Jamie's your man. He's a bestselling stand-
up comedian, a Grammy-winning singer/songwriter, and the
kind of Oscar-winning actor Quentin Tarantino begs to be his
leading man. He started out as a choirboy and classical pianist
before working his way from the comedy circuit into TV and the
Hollywood elite. He's the small-town boy who also throws the best
parties in town. On his balcony. Where P. Diddy and Kanye West
just happen to be playing some tunes.

Chadwick Boseman

What's great about Chad isn't just his hotness (undeniable), but also his fearlessness. He's taken on and nailed the roles of two legends: Jackie Robinson and James Brown. As James Brown, he had the husky voice and the moves—he mastered the splits, the spins, and even the Mashed Potato. And now, just to cement his stardom, he's Black Panther—king of the unconquerable African nation of Wakanda and Marvel's first black superhero. And superheroes don't get much hotter than Chad. He's got the crooked smile, the quiet charisma, and the lovely eyebrows (check them out and tell me you don't want to stroke them). Oh, Chadwick . . . it feels like you're finally getting the attention you deserve.

Paul Rudd

He's Hollywood's most loveable man. He just looks so nice, with his boyish smile and twinkly eyes, as if he could be your boyfriend, best friend, and shoulder to cry on all rolled into one. And he likes milky tea, which somehow makes him seem nicer still. You might know him from *Friends*, or Apatow comedies, or as Ant-Man, but really, you have to LOVE Paul Rudd for one reason, and one reason alone: his role in *Clueless*, one of THE BEST romantic comedies of ALL TIME. He plays Josh, who kisses Cher at the top of the stairs in a way that makes you want to rewatch the scene a million times. If you haven't already seen this film, watch it, and then you too will love lovely Paul Rudd.

Jamie Dornan

We could talk about his role in *Fifty Shades of Grey*, but of course he's done other work. He's also one of the highest-paid male models, with a body known as "The Golden Torso," just like we saw in *Fifty Shades of Grey*. But of course there's much more to him than that. He's also a musician who has a lilting Northern Irish accent to melt your heart and lovely chocolatey brown eyes (put to excellent use in *Fifty Shades of Grey*). He can be versatile, too: He plays a psychopath in *The Fall* with a really complex character, just like Christian in *Fifty Shades of Grey*. Okay, so it's impossible not to think about Jamie and *Fifty Shades of Grey* at the same time, but the excellent news is, there are still two more *Fifty Shades* films to come.
#bringiton

Channing Tatum

Channing is the HUNKSOME heartthrob of the moment. He danced his way to fame in *Step Up* and then cemented his stardom by making a film about his past as a stripper (see *Magic Mike*). And just to prove his versatility, he put on an incredible performance in *Foxcatcher*. In fact, the list of his talents is a bit endless, so here are just TEN REASONS TO LOVE CHANNING TATUM: 1. his amazing shoulders, 2. he can really act, 3. his amazing shoulders, 4. his dancing skills, 5. he's the PERFECT husband, 6. he's so cool, he now does Coen Brothers and Tarantino films, 7. he loves cake, 8. he had a childhood imaginary friend, 9. he starred in Ricky Martin's "She Bangs" video, 10. his amazing shoulders.

Kit Harington

This is how important Kit Harington is to the world: There are Twitter feeds dedicated to his beard status; entire websites are on Beard Watch, providing day-by-day updates. And when he does shave it off, grown women cry. That's how emotionally invested people are in Kit's follicles. As Jon Snow in *Game of Thrones*, this brown-eyed, baby-faced beauty of a man is contracted to keep his beard and long, flowing locks. If they go, it's a sign he might be killed off. So far, so good—it looks like the sword-wielding, brooding hunkster is set to stay on our screens for a while longer. Phew! Where would we be without our weekly swoon over the Lord Commander of the Beard?

Will Smith

First you go through the *Fresh Prince of Bel Air* stage. It's like
a teen rite of passage. This is when you think you want to be
Will, before discovering you can't rap or carry off the sideways
baseball cap look. Then there are the blockbusters—*Men in
Black, I Am Legend,* and *Independence Day*—in which you
discover that Will is the only man who can save the planet
in moments of apocalyptic crisis and/or alien invasion whilst
simultaneously admiring his incredibly toned physique. Finally, you
get to fall fully in love with Will in *Hitch* and *Focus,* watching him
be a heartthrob. And then you can rejoice in your devotion by
starting all over again with *Fresh Prince*.

Brad Pitt

Brad Pitt started out in pretty-boy roles (think *Thelma and Louise*—yes, THAT scene, with Brad in the cowboy hat, a battered pair of jeans, and nothing else, looking so good it's no wonder Geena Davis kept fluffing her lines), then in beautiful roles, striding about like a young Robert Redford in *A River Runs Through It*. Then he turns his versatile hands to tongue-in-cheek movies like *Ocean's Eleven* and generally being very cool with George Clooney. Then, before you know it, he's a Hollywood big-hitter, gaining nominations for his lead roles and producing Academy Award-winning films like *12 Years a Slave*. So Brad, here's to you, so much more than just a pretty face (but what a face . . .).

Daniel Dae Kim

If you like men with jet-black hair, fathomless eyes, slashing cheekbones, and amazing muscles, then Daniel Dae Kim is probably the best Hollywood go-to heartthrob. You might know him from *Lost* or *Hawaii Five-0*, or for being clever (wearing glasses, talking a lot of science) in *Insurgent*. But as Daniel himself has said, where are the Asian American romantic or lead roles? Any casting directors out there reading this? Because we're listening, Daniel, and we agree. Someone, please, please cast Daniel Dae Kim as the romantic leading man. *People* magazine named him Sexiest Man Alive. What more do you need? We'll be very grateful.

Dev Patel

Dev, Dev, Dev . . . you might be off doing amazing things now, but for us you'll always be Jamal Malik, the hero of *Slumdog Millionaire*, sharing THAT KISS at the train station at the end, like the teen dream of hope. Ooh, except that now the loveable Dev has got new luscious long locks and *GQ*-style facial hair, perfectly framing his huge, chocolatey brown eyes. And he's broader and . . . well . . . a lot manlier. And in *Lion*, you suddenly realize that underneath all those tracksuits, he possesses a body that is positively Hemsworthian. Dev Patel is not a cute goofball anymore but a rare thing—a total hunk, WITH SOUL. Arise, Dev Patel, new heartthrob of Hollywood.

Joe Manganiello

For four years, he was a mega-buff werewolf in *True Blood*, playing possibly the best on-screen werewolf ever (excepting Michael J. Fox, obviously). He is six foot five with the most incredible muscles, which were perfected still further for *Magic Mike*. He looks so amazing in that film, director Stephen Soderbergh thought his physique MUST HAVE BEEN COMPUTER GENERATED. So, yes. WOW. But Joe works hard at his muscles. He's so into muscle-building, he's written a book about it. You can buy it, and then in six weeks you too can look like a werewolf. Or you could just buy the book and spend your time feasting your eyes on Joe Manganiello in all his insanely hot glory.

Eddie Redmayne

What is it about Eddie Redmayne? With his auburn hair, green eyes, and dusting of freckles, Eddie is beautiful—strikingly beautiful (no wonder he was snapped up by Burberry). He's massively intelligent—check. He makes astounding films—check. He's stylish and courteous—check. He's amazingly well-dressed—check. He can sing (*Les Misérables*)—check. He's posh (just in case you're into that sort of thing)—check. All sounding a bit too perfect? But then there's that Oscar speech, where he comes over all bashful and charmingly British, fumbling for the right words. And . . . we're only stopping here because we're running out of space. Oh, Eddie.

Henry Cavill

For all his square-jawed poster-perfect good looks and muscled physique, Henry Cavill spent years in Hollywood not getting parts (he missed out on Pattinson's role in *Harry Potter*, on a part in *Twilight*, and on playing James Bond). And then along came *Man of Steel*, and Cavill nailed it . . . in more ways than one. He got so big and muscular during filming, he even split his Clark Kent costume. As for the superhero outfit, he can pull off a skin-tight, electric blue leotard with ease. And this is from the guy who used to be bullied at school. Well, turning into the ultimate superhero is the perfect revenge on school bullies everywhere. Oh, that and being voted World's Sexiest Man.

Javier Bardem

With those eyes, that tall, square frame, and deep Spanish purr, Bardem exudes lazy sex appeal. But Bardem's not just an incredible physical presence, he's also one of THE GREATS, up there with Al Pacino and Jack Nicholson. Film directors write parts with him in mind. He's been equally convincing as a gay Cuban poet, a quadriplegic, an assassin, and a Columbian lothario. He's also arguably been the best Bond villain ever. And even though he's incredible playing romantic leads, you might want to avert your eyes when he's doing his serial killer thing. And yet he can go from that to brooding sex symbol in a heartbeat. A prince of an actor. A lion among men.

Jason Momoa

Look at Jason Momoa and you may feel slightly faint. Or suffer palpitations, because he's SMOKIN' HOT. It gets worse when you add in his voice . . . deep, sexy, and gravelly with a hint of honey (you see what he does to people? You start off talking about his voice and end up sounding like you're describing a fine wine). You may know him as Khal Drogo in *Game of Thrones*, or as Aquaman in *Justice League*. If you haven't heard of him, let us describe him for you: He's a six-foot-five, tanned, mountain of a man with an amazing eyebrow scar, a tattoo of shark teeth on his forearm, and beach-wave-long locks. Actually, we're going to have to stop there . . . any more and it's going to bring on those palpitations.

Matthew McConaughey

Laid-back, Texan drawl, sun-kissed golden skin, curls, sea blue eyes, washboard abs, the flash of white teeth in that killer smile . . . what's not to love about Matthew McConaughey? For a while there, he was the KING of romantic comedies. Oozing his southern charm across the genre, running around with his shirt off, falling in love, and perfecting the dramatic "take me back" scene so that by the end you were always shouting "YES! TAKE HIM BACK!" because he's so insanely GORGEOUS. And then suddenly a new Matthew McConaughey appeared, who keeps his shirt on and instead of wooing women he takes on Oscar-worthy and deeply moving roles, and you realize this is one incredibly talented man. Sigh.

Leonardo DiCaprio

Oh, Leo! We were there with you on the balcony, being Juliet to your Romeo. We were there with you on the *Titanic,* as you slipped beneath the icy waters. We flew round the world with you in *Catch Me if You Can* and watched you go wild on Wall Street as you grew from a beautiful boy into a handsome man. You can get away with goatees and man-buns. Even with all your wild ways, we've also seen you dedicate yourself to the art of acting and film (jumping in and out of icy rivers, sleeping in animal carcasses), and tirelessly campaigning for the environment as well as being one of the Hollywood greats. We're glad they still make them like you, Leo.

Johnny Depp

Johnny, Johnny . . . so beautiful. His eyes are liquid pools of onyx. Those to-die-for cheekbones, black hair, and that pout . . . you embody the rebel, the misfit, the outsider. Ever since you sang on our screens in *Cry-Baby*, with your tight white T-shirt and your tear drop tattoo, we've loved you. Then you won us all over again with your whimsy in *Benny & Joon*. Okay, so you've been around for a little while now, but there's a reason we stayed loyal. You have sad, sexy, sensitive, and mysterious down to perfection. Even when you have blades for fingers or you're a drunk, louche pirate captain with an artistic flair for eyeliner, you're irresistible.

Bradley Cooper

In his early Hollywood years, no one wanted him. The only roles he was offered were the sidekicks and the jerks. HOW TIMES HAVE CHANGED. Now Bradley Cooper is considered one of the finest actors and sexiest men on the planet: the amazing, crazy, sea green eyes, the lupine grin, the chiselled jaw. You might have first noticed him in *The Hangover*, playing his role with suave assuredness, but then in *Silver Linings Playbook*—that's where you fall in love with him and realize there's more to him than a one-dimensional hunkfest. #massiveswoonalert

Ryan Reynolds

Definitely, Maybe and *The Proposal* are two romcoms that shouldn't work, but do, because of Ryan. And then his big moment came with *Deadpool* (which he cowrote and starred in). It's fast, funny, and subversive. It smashed the box office, and now he's a total Hollywood superstar. So what is it that makes Ryan Reynolds so hot? It's not just his looks (gorgeous) or his success (massive). It has to be the fact that he's funny. So, so funny. He made a foul-mouthed comic book anti-hero into his biggest success story. This is also a man who loves DIY, changes diapers, and laughs at the superficiality of fame. That's just very, very loveable. Oh yes, we heart you, Ryan Reynolds.

Jake Gyllenhaal

If you go for the quiet, sensitive, soul-searching types, then Jake Gyllenhaal is probably the heartthrob for you. He has the looks of a movie star—eyes like twin pools of blue, a chiseled jawline, and even a lovely, soft beard (okay, the "soft" part hasn't been tested, but it looks soft)—but he takes on roles that are the opposite of that: outsiders, loners, and characters who don't quite follow the social norms. He's the kind of actor who transforms himself physically and emotionally for his roles. He chooses films only on the basis of whether or not they inspire him creatively. He's an intellectual and an activist who wants people to focus on the internal. Which we will. Right after we've finished admiring those lovely eyes . . .

Dwayne Johnson

AKA "The Rock," Dwayne Johnson is a mountain of a man—he's six foot five inches and 252 pounds with bulging biceps, a chest like a bull's, and a body covered with tattoos. Wrestler turned actor, Johnson is the go-to action hero of the moment, the real deal, Schwarzenegger and Stallone rolled into one. He was one of the most successful wrestlers in history, with 17 championship reigns, was Hollywood's highest earner in 2016, and was recently voted Sexiest Man Alive by *People* magazine. He's worked hard to get where he is; from football player to wrestler to Hollywood action hero. It all sounds like a movie. So where does he go from here? Next stop, the White House?

Michael B. Jordan

You have to start with his role as Wallace in *The Wire*. He was only 15, but it BROKE OUR HEARTS when his character was killed off. Okay, if you haven't seen *The Wire*, none of this will make sense, except that even then, Jordan had the power to make you fall for him. Now he's hot Hollywood property after commanding the screen in *Fruitvale Station* and then hypnotizing us all with his biceps in *Creed*. Actually, it wasn't just his biceps. It was also his back muscles. And his abs. Basically, he was so ridiculously ripped it was almost too much to take in. And now he's bulking up again to play the villain in the new *Black Panther* film. P.S. You should know that the "B" in his name stands for Bakari, which means "promising" (so, so true).

Chris Pratt

Oh, Chris Pratt. He does funny and sexy in the best combo since apple pie and ice cream—hot and delicious and comforting all at the same time. First, he's all soft and cute as goofball Andy in *Parks and Recreation*. Then, suddenly he's getting his abs out as an action-star hunk, leading the Marvel mega-hit *Guardians of the Galaxy*, and Indiana-Dinosaur-Jones styling it in *Jurassic World*. Offscreen, he's busy being part of Hollywood's most adorable fun couple and looking like Hot Dad of the Year with his son Jack. Must stop looking at photos of Chris Pratt with his son. Or the one with the motorcycle from *Jurassic World*. Or the naked torso shot from *Guardians of the Galaxy*. KNEES. FEEL. WEAK.

Tom Hardy

There's something a bit wild about Tom Hardy. Maybe it's the chameleon-esque way he glides from one (frequently menacing) role to the next, or the intensity he brings to each part, whether he's playing a solider, a violent criminal, a wild-haired woodsman, or Mad Max. But that's all part of his rough, ready, and ruggedly handsome appeal. And then to offset it . . . there's the big softy side. He once said he was "as masculine as an eggplant." Take his love of dogs—and by love, we really mean LOVE (he even brought his dog on the red carpet). Or the rap he did on behalf of his baby son. Beneath that hard exterior, he has a heart of gold . . . and maybe that's the secret of his sexiness.

Robert Downey Jr.

He's one of the highest-paid stars in Hollywood (not that we're interested in him for his money). Oh, no. Downey Jr. is the one that brings that something extra to a film, whether he's doing an uncannily good Chaplin or packing a punch in *Iron Man*. This is a man who defines the meaning of screen presence—all eyes are drawn to him. He's handsome, even elegant, but there's something rough around the edges that makes him even sexier than a run-of-the-mill square-jawed hunk. And then when he speaks . . . he does sassy and witty and calm and manic energy in a fascinating mix that doesn't age.

Alden Ehrenreich

He has one of the best starting-out stories: Steven Spielberg spotted Alden in a video shown at a friend's bar mitzvah, and liked what he saw so much that he recommended him to his friend Francis Ford Coppola. It wasn't long before Alden was starring alongside the likes of George Clooney in a Coen Brothers film as a Texan cowboy who is really, really good at horse tricks. Next up, he's going to be the young Han Solo. Couple that with the fact that he looks a lot like a young Leonardo DiCaprio with the soulful stare of Johnny Depp, and gets rave reviews for every film he makes. That definitely makes Alden one to watch.